TINY- RANNOSAURUS

By
Nick Ward

Albury Children's

Many, many years ago...

when the world was a wild and dangerous place...

... when everywhere was covered
with volcanoes and jungles...

... and when fierce dinosaurs ruled the earth...

...the fiercest dinosaur

Carythosaurus

Apotasaurus

Iguanadon

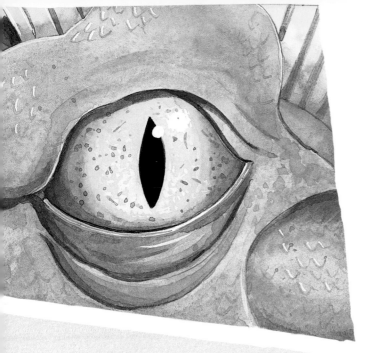

# of all was...

Triceratops

...Tinyrannosaurus
(wrecks).

Because he wasn't as big as some of the other dinosaurs,
Tiny had to be especially fierce to make up for it.

So he had learned to
roar the loudest roar...

ROAR!

... clash his jaws
the hardest...

SLAM!

... and pull the fiercest faces.

He was the loudest, hardest,
fiercest and grumpiest
little dinosaur ever!

Even as a baby,
Tiny had been a handful.

He stamped and
growled and would
kick up a storm.

But today...

...Tiny was even grumpier than normal.
He had an awful toothache,
which was not good news,
as everyone knows dinosaurs
love to **EAT!**

Dino
POPS
Tasty bits
of gravel

"I'm famished," grumbled Tiny as he sat down to breakfast and bit down hard on his favourite food.

"Ouch!" he cried. "My tooth!"

"Oh dear," said his mum. "We'd better go and have that tooth pulled out."

"No way!" cried Tinyrannosaurus, and off he went to find some friends.

Tiny stomped through the jungle in a grumpy mood. His tooth ached and his tummy was empty.

Then, just around the corner, he came upon Triceratops eating in a clearing.

"**Food!**" smiled Tiny. He roared his loudest roar. He pulled his fiercest face and bellowed...

Charge!

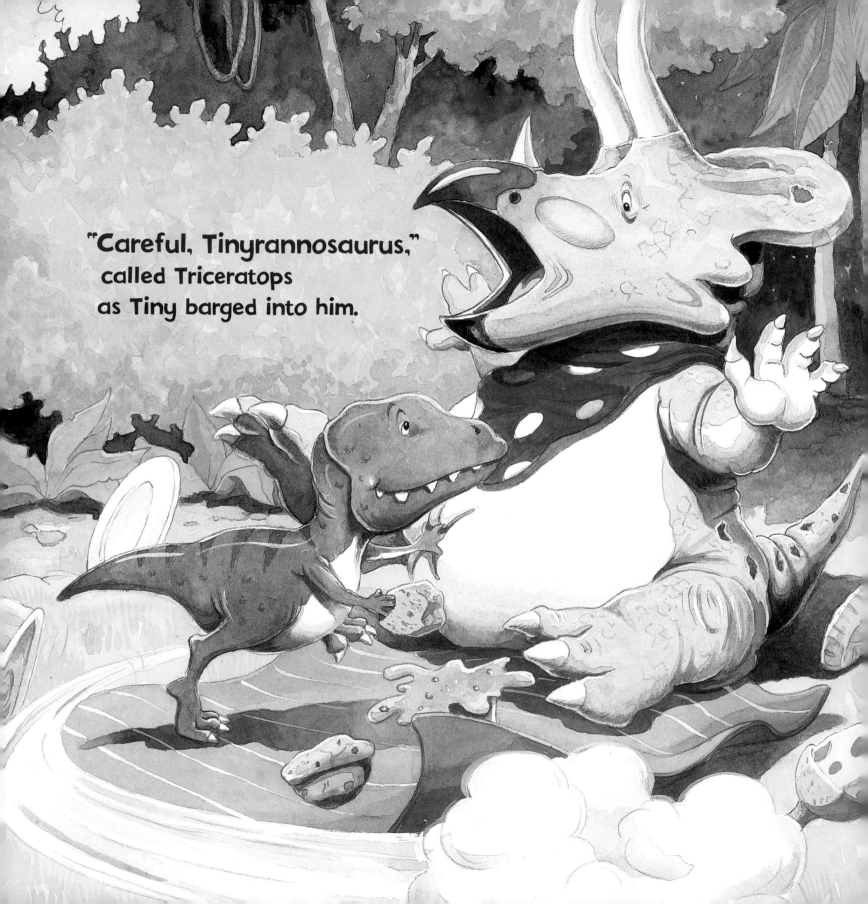

"Careful, Tinyrannosaurus," called Triceratops as Tiny barged into him.

Tiny stomped down to the river.

"I'm starving," he moaned,
and then he smelt fresh berries...

... and followed the scent
to a group of Apatosauruses.

"Charge!"
he yelled
and stormed
towards them...

... picking up
 a huge bunch of berries
 and slamming shut
  his mighty jaws.

"Ow! Ow! Ouch!" he cried. "My tooth!"

"Oh dear," said the Apatosaurus. "Perhaps you should see about having it removed."

"I won't have it removed!" sobbed Tiny and stomped off up the nearest volcano...

Food!

...where he found his best friend Vilo C Raptor who was eating an apple.

"**Food!**" thundered Tiny, roaring his loudest roar and pulling his fiercest face.

"**Stop, Tiny, STOP!**" yelped Vilo.

And as Tiny got within nipping distance of the apple, he **CLASHED** his mighty jaws...

"YeoOoowwwwwouch!"

howled Tiny.

"What's the matter with you?"
munched Vilo.

"I'm sorry, Vilo," said Tiny,
"But I'm so hungry, and I've
got a terrible toothache."

"Then perhaps
you'd better go
and have it
taken out,"
said Vilo.

"NO!" screamed Tiny

"I WON'T HAVE IT REMOVED!"

... and stamping and roaring
and growling and grimacing...

... Tinyrannosaurus kicked up
a **REAL STORM**,
until the clouds churned
and lightning flashed everywhere.

But when the dust settled, Tiny still had a terrible toothache and an empty tummy.

"Oh dear," he sighed. "Perhaps I had better have it removed."

"Open wide," said Dr Stegosaurus peering inside Tiny's mouth.

Tap, tap, tap.
"How does that feel?" he asked.

"Much better, thank you," said Tiny.

"Good. You should be able to eat something now," smiled the Dentist.

"I can?!" said Tiny,
and jumped up,
mouth open,
and went
CHOMP!

For Mickybrockosaurus,

from one old dinosaur to another!

N.W.

Published by Albury Books in 2014
Albury Court, Albury, Thame, OX9 2LP, United Kingdom

Text © Nick Ward • Illustrations © Nick Ward
The rights of Nick Ward to be identified as the author and
illustrator have been asserted by them in accordance with the
Copyright, Designs and Patents Act, 1988

ISBN 978-1-909958-58-6 (hardback)
ISBN 978-1-909958-37-1 (paperback)

A CIP catalogue record for this book is available from the
British Library 10 9 8 7 6 5 4 3
Printed in Malaysia